Sue Wood

The Legend of
Miri the Manger Cat

Susan K. Woodall

Published by Susan K. Woodall

Published in the United States of America by Susan K. Woodall, 2010

To contact the author or arrange a booksigning or fundraising event:

mirithemangercat@aol.com

ISBN 978-1-4507-4507-9

Printing by Blurb, Inc.
blurb.com

I dedicate this book to my grandmother, Elsie,

and her daughter, my mother, Fran.

Both brought to me the wonder of the world

through stories

that live in my heart today.

"I loved
The Legend of Miri the Manger Cat.
The author certainly has a way of telling a story!"

Reverend Steve Ranson
Minister of Hazelwood Christian Church
Hazelwood, Indiana

The Legend of Miri the Manger Cat is a family experience, to be shared with loved ones during special reading times.

Written in the oral folk tradition, grandparents and parents can read it aloud to the children 'round the fire, and create a new Christmas family tradition. *Miri* can also be cherished all times of the year, by all ages.

Although designed for daily chapter readings, it can be read at one time. Your imaginations are your wings as you supplement it with family drawing sessions of the characters, questions about the nativity or the Bible, directed discussions, even in children's Sunday school classes, or design activities around Miri that are just plain fun!
It is time.

About the author

Sue Woodall is a veteran teacher of thirty-seven years, with teaching experiences from elementary to university. She taught high school at Clinton, Austin, and Greencastle, Indiana, Winter Haven, Florida, and, as a Fulbright exchange teacher, at Cambridge, Ontario. She also taught at Indiana State University and Ivy Tech College.

Although Sue has enjoyed teaching psychology, English, Latin, drama, and courses for gifted and talented students, as well as being a school librarian for many years, her first love centers around storytelling—myths, legends, the oral folk tradition, children's literature, creative writing, and writing stories herself.

Her love for storytelling began in childhood listening to folk tales and family lore related by her beloved mother and grandmother. This love deepened with her exposure to folklore and creative writing through her university years. Sue began using her own tales, not only as stories for the classroom, but as bedtime stories for her "jewels", daughters Jamie and Jessie, alias Jamie Baby and Sea Biscuit.

After attaining a master's degree in library science, the library became Sue's castle filled with wealth. She traveled extensively as a tour guide abroad and won awards for creative teaching. More and more stories were added to her treasure troves. Certainly her love for a story was not squelched when she married her husband, Mike, a former English teacher with a minor in folklore. A real joy was to bring students to the creative writing stage, and see them blossom with their own narratives.

The theft of a library therapy cat that Sue personally trained and the long search to find that special cat exposed her to the world of homeless and abused cats and brought her into cat rescue. The two loves blended in Sue's writing; thus the birth of Miri, the Manger Cat.

Foreword

My dear daughters, my dear hearts, Jamie Baby
and Sea Biscuit, you ask me why our Joanie is so
very special, and why we call her a manger cat.

This "cat tale" began in ancient times, in times
before written storybooks existed and before
mothers in pink housecoats prepared their
beloved children for gentle sleep in soft little bunk
beds.

It is not just Joanie's story, but the story of many
other cats. Joanie's ancestors, her family from
two thousand years ago until now—very special
cats, very special stories, all blending together,
and finally, Joanie, who found her way into our
lives.

Hundreds and hundreds and hundreds of years
ago....

Are you ready to hear my story? It is one that has

passed from my mother to me, her mother to her, and back as long as anyone in our family can ever remember. It is a most special story, so special I will put it all together for you in our bedtime stories. Then I will create for you a present, a book which tells the saga of Miri, so that all may know.

Sit with me as each day becomes eve, as we prepare to snuggle in our beds and rest for each new day. You will know the whole legend within a few evenings. Listen well.

It is time.

Chapter I

Once upon a time, many more years ago than the
roses and lavender that have blossomed in my
summer garden, in a far-away land of sand and
sun, a little cat named Miri lived in the tiny town of
Bethlehem.

Miri's mom, Lolly, had raised her litter of kittens in
the haystacks of the old stable near the Inn.
Isaac, the Innkeeper, called it his own manger
because in the stable he kept his cow, Momo; two

lambs, Taz and Bobo; a goat, Kibiddle; and the donkey, Fleabit.

Sometimes the big gray-and-white rabbit, Tippy, would hop in to keep warm or rest for a while. The smell of fresh hay and all the animal smells mixed with an old smell of wet dampness, for the manger had originally been a cave.

Lolly left her five kittens as soon as they could scamper about the manger on their own to find bits of the food Isaac left for the other animals. She loved her boys, Ruckey and Zori, and her girls, Miri, Bitsy, and Lil Bit, but she wanted great new adventures in the outside world.
The kittens missed their mother. They were sad, and huddled together in their bed of straw until they became hungry.

Ruckey, the shiny black leader of the litter, grew restless, and said to his brother and sisters, "Do not worry. We are together, and will take care of each other. It is time."
His bright green eyes shined with determination

as he told his brothers and sisters there would be no problems, as long as they stayed in the manger together. They followed as he led them to the animals' bowls filled with bits of leftover food from the Inn.

As they ate, they rallied, and played around the hooves of the other creatures, who the kittens knew would never hurt them. The kittens had grown up around them, and all were part of a big family held together by the good, smiling Isaac. Even grumpy donkey Fleabit was really gentle inside.

Yet soon their new life changed because of Isaac himself. Isaac's daughter, Jessa, was having her tenth birthday. Since Isaac had many mouths to feed, and was very generous to not only the animals, but also any humans who needed his help, he had no money for a special present.

Upon entering the manger to give his animals their supper, he spied the fluffy white, sky-blue-eyed princesses, Bitsy and Lil Bit. They were delicately washing themselves while sunning near the manger's entrance.

"What quiet, sweet, beautiful kittens! I bet they would be great cuddly companions for my daughter. What prizes for her birthday!"

Bitsy and Lil Bit let him scoop them up in his big arms and carry them inside to the cozy hearth of the Inn. They never were sorry, for they became the joys of Jessa's life. They slept on her bed, and became her greatest friends. They grew chubby on the choicest morsels offered by guests, and they purred contentedly, often on the laps of the visiting guests. They were admired often as the best of cats, as the cuddly darlings they were. This world was theirs, and they soon forgot their former lives and hardships.

Zori was the wild one, who delighted in attacking brooms and hay mounds. It seemed that he constantly fought imaginary foes, jumped from the highest "mountains", and won every battle. He was born with a bad eye, but used his good one to conquer every challenge he found. No fear or sadness in his heart; he enjoyed each encounter, each day. He never surrendered.

One day he discovered a wondrously huge beetle, scurrying across the ground in front of the manger. He accepted this new mission with zeal and immense curiosity, jumping in one bound to the outside of the manger. He extended his paw over and over to the beetle, stopping it in every attempt of flight it tried.

Jacob, the baker, watched. About to begin again his long journey home, he rested while smiling at Zori's antics. He found himself forgetting his headache, sore aching legs, and the tiring, bad day he had with complaining customers at his bakery—those to whom he was nothing but a grouchy, useless, penny-pinching old man, he thought.

"What a silly creature, such a little thing of bright orange swirls and snowy white patches, like the sweets I make for holidays. Perhaps he needs a home. He can be the guardian for my bakery storeroom."

Jacob did not know that he needed Zori as much as Zori needed him.

After a short time at the bakery, Zori moved from the storeroom to keep Jacob company while he baked, then explored the floor when customers came in. Soon Zori had his own cushion near the bakery counter. He would jump up, greet, and inspect each customer. Shaking hands with each buyer with his outstretched paw, inspecting baskets, dusting shelves, Zori became a star, and a great attraction for the customers.

 Soon Jacob was slinging Zori on his shoulder to take him home, which somehow became a shorter walk with Zori as ally. Zori soon had his own chair and plate at the house table. Each morning Jacob would again carry him to the bakery on his shoulder. Once there, Zori would begin his daily job of inspecting the bakery, greeting customers, and assisting Jacob with the baking.

Soon no one could think of the baker without thinking of his assistant, Zori. Business became brisk. As more and more customers came in just to see Zori, Jacob began to smile often, and laugh out loud with his customer friends.

He looked forward to his days at the bakery with the cat. He never knew what antics the cat would provide to cause the laughter that made him forget his pain and age. Customers proclaimed the cat was magical. Not only did Zori make Jacob feel young again, but he made Jacob friendly with each customer, and even a better baker!

Zori's brightness was not just in his orange color, but in his playful love of life and affection for Jacob. Zori filled Jacob's empty heart with love, the real magic. The bad eye? Jacob never saw it, just as Zori never saw Jacob's old age.

Oh, but I am sorry, Dear Hearts. I told you I was

going to tell of the first Manger Cat, Miri. Instead, I got derailed! I told you about what happened to the others. Yet what miracle could possibly be better than that of the father's love for his daughter, a girl's love for her pets, or a kitten bringing an old man back to life and laughter?

You shall soon find out....

It is time.

Chapter II

When Bitsy and Lil Bit went to Jessa, and Zori romped into the arms of Jacob, only two kittens of Lolly's litter remained…the strong Ruckey and timid Miri.

Ruckey took care of his sister by keeping her warm against his fur during the cold nights, and giving her the best of the food left by Isaac. Sometimes there was not enough food, and Ruckey would have to search outside at night, when the streets were less busy.

Miri thought Ruckey would be there forever for her, and gladly let him give her the most food. She also let him pick the best spots in the manger to sleep. This was her favorite time. As all the animals slept, and she and Ruckey curled up together, it seemed that a special calm came over the manger. All were family.

In the morning, Miri awoke to the rustling movement and the vocal sounds of the others, all blended together. The gentle lowing of Momo, the cow, the anxious baa-ing of Bobo and Taz, and even donkey Fleabit, who kept time with his snorts and hooves—all was music to Miri. Kibiddle the goat chewed most seriously. Tippy the rabbit quietly hopped about looking for bits of grain. It was comfortable. It was home.

Even with her mom, other sisters and brother gone, Ruckey and Miri were together, safe in the place they had always known, with the ones who knew them. Miri was content.

Ruckey was the serious one. Sometimes he would sit for hours, never moving, looking straight ahead, as if he were solving all the problems in his world. Since Miri was most often with him, she too became quiet, yet inside she felt she really had no special qualities at all. She did not have Ruckey's strength, nor did she play hero like her brother Zori. She certainly did not purr or look beautiful like her sisters.

Miri was an ordinary brown-striped tiger cat, with a patch of white around her mouth, light brown-orange fur on her belly, and long tufts of fur on her ears. She had soft creme circles around each eye, and black eyeliner stretching to her cheeks, like an Egyptian queen. A black fur, necklace-like ring stretched thoroughly around her neck.

Her most lovely qualities were the thick, black, beautiful stripes on her soft, dark-brown fur (matching on both hind legs as they swirled delightfully down her striped pajama body); the shiny black thick line running down her whole back; and the huge, round, golden sun eyes that had the same serious glance as Ruckey's.

Miri was not aware that these features were lovely; she only saw herself as a plain, dull-colored little cat. She also never knew how very striking her eyes were. Those eyes that seemed to stare at whatever she looked at… as if she, too, were looking into the very souls of others.

Yet Miri never did feel special. Without Bit and Bitsy's glamour, Zori's zest for life, or Ruckey's depth of thought, she felt the least one of the litter. Thank goodness she had Ruckey.

Ruckey's fur was as completely black as the darkest evening, so it was easier for him to scout at night when humans were sleeping. Only his huge grass-green eyes could be seen glowing, as he searched for food outside. One night, when Miri was sleeping, he went to find breakfast for the following morning. He did not return.

When Miri awoke, she looked everywhere in the manger for Ruckey, even daring to pop outside the manger, where it was so busy with people during the day. After days of looking and waiting, squeaking her little mews, and not finding Ruckey, she became even quieter than usual. She curled into a ball, refusing to eat, drink, or even acknowledge the presence of other animals.

She stayed in the same spot near the entrance of the manger. If she moved, she would perhaps miss Ruckey's sound if he cried out for her from the street. Days passed. Miri became tired, hungry, and weak. She did not care. She was alone. She had nothing. She had no one. Everyone had left her because they did not want her. She was not special.

In this darkest time for Miri, she did not know what was ahead of her. She had no faith. She could not know that faith brings miracles. Yet even so, a miracle was waiting for her, traveling to her town, on its way. It was a miracle for all of us. This miracle would soon especially need Miri's faith in action.
It still needs our faith in action today.

It is time.

Chapter III

That night was Miri's darkest—losing all of her family and feeling no one wanted her. She was hungry, alone, and frightened.

Then Miri dreamed. In this dream, a golden glow suddenly surrounded her thin body, and immediately strengthened her. She no longer felt hungry or scared. A gentle voice—even more beautiful than all the animal lullabies or her mother's old croons of love—sang to her in a starlit language that only cats can understand. Miri felt love, acceptance, joy. The magical song told Miri that she was special, needed, and cherished. That no one else was Miri, and that Miri was exactly in the place she needed to be. That she was not alone.

Miri basked in the sun of total peace as the voice as fragile and enchanting as hummingbird wings trilled that she should not give up. Miri calmly listened, enchanted, then fell into the best sleep she had since she lost Ruckey.

Miri awoke, stretched, and realized she was no longer tired. Miri felt strength and energy. She no longer felt alone. Something special was going to happen. She waited for something to happen. She waited for something to change in the manger.

"It is time," she thought.

She quickly lapped up some water and even dared go outside to find a piece of bread. Jacob's stale bread, dropped as he took it home, lugging little companion Zori on his shoulder.

Miri was confident, on her own. It was new to her. She always needed someone else in her life to take care of her. She was indeed a scaredy cat, she thought to herself! Ruckey had been her caregiver and protector. The girls Bitsy and Lil Bit were wanted for their charm. Zori had the personality and the bright orange swirls. Ruckey had the natural wisdom and leadership….

What did Miri have? Why was she needed? What did she have to give? Why did she have this special dream, she, a plain, ordinary brown little cat? Who could possibly love her the way she felt loved in the dream, for herself? The dream lullaby told her that she was different. It made her feel good about herself. What did it mean?

Miri was curled up high in the haystack, trying, in the silence, to dream back the sweet memories of the dream song. She wanted to hear it again, and feel so loved again.

She awoke to the sounds of a restless Momo, complaining as she chewed her cud. Fleabit was kicking his water bucket with his hooves, and pronouncing loud he-haws to accompany Kibiddle the goat's sour notes. Only the lambs Taz and Bobo seemed quietly listening. More sounds….

Now, what never happens…human sounds, sounds other than Isaac, their feeder. More sounds, as the giant of a man leads in a small wisp of a woman (as humans go), on a donkey.

Miri's life would never be the same.

It is time.

Chapter IV

Frightened by the presence of humans, Miri had
jumped up higher into the hay mounds and
peered down at them, watching their every move.
She usually felt threatened by unfamiliar humans
outside the manger, but with these humans she
felt that same lovely calmness brought to her in
her dream, as if they were a continuing part of the
dream, a part of the voice.

"Mary, are you all right?" asked the bearded giant

in the rough brown homespun robes.

"Yes, Joseph, but I must rest. I thank God that Isaac is allowing us to stay in his stable."

With every move as soft as a leaf falling gently from a tree, Joseph lifted Mary from the back of the donkey, as if she were the most valued prize on the earth.

As Miri watched in wonder, somehow she knew they would bring her no harm. When Mary talked, again Miri heard the soft loving tones she heard in her dream. Something was about to happen that would change the world. They would be part of it. The humans also knew, and waited.

Hope has come to Miri in spite of her aloneness. Her energy was now different. It seemed to double because of hope, because of faith in the promises given to her in the dream. She was renewed; she felt needed and strong, and these feelings were tied to these humans. She would wait and watch over them.

Hope and faith have worked together, and become one in Miri's heart. Her life would now change for the better. She felt as beautiful as she had felt in her dream.

Until now, she dealt with humans in the least way possible, even running from them. She especially feared them after Ruckey was gone. Now they, too, were waiting for something to happen. They could no longer be avoided; they were here in her own home, and yet their presence made her feel safe.

Miri wanted to protect the humans, since they seemed so much in need. They slept with the animals, huddled in old cloaks in the same straw Miri used for her bed. They ate little.

Then, in the night air, strange sounds pierced the silence—from Mary. Joseph comforted her in a quiet, loving voice, encouraging her, always staying by her side, giving her small sips of water. Miri's eyes watched both of them working together in the night. She felt the goodness coming from the couple working as a team. Miri wished she had the courage to go to them, to sit nearby, to give the woman comfort in a purr, or even dare to be near enough to be touched. She edged out of the darkness, nearer the oil lamp light, nearer Mary.

"Look, Joseph," Mary spoke softly in a moment of rest, "a little cat, like the one I had when I was a little girl. She means no harm; she almost acts as if she wants to help us. I think she feels my pain and wants to take it away…such a little cat, but she dares to come near us. Look how amazing her eyes are…sun-gold, watching, seeing, trying to understand. She looks so wise and she is so beautiful, like a little tiger."

Her soft-sweet words soothed Miri like a soft Momma tongue washing her when she was a kitten. An embrace of love.

"She is good luck for us." Mary managed a smile for Miri before she set to her task again.

Joseph quickly agreed with Mary, concerned that she was giving too much energy and strength to the conversation, but realizing that Mary seemed to get more energy, more determination.

"Yes, Mary, she is truly sent by the angels, for she has given you joy and strength. She seems to know us."

As Joseph directed his words to Mary, he looked into the golden bright eyes of Miri, and seemed to recognize something in her, something of the same calm he felt after a dream of his own, when angels had told him of a special miracle.

So they continued, the three of them. Joseph making Mary as comfortable as he could, while the little cat of the bright eyes and serious attitude watched the couple's activities of the night.

"Here, have some water, Mary. Rest while you can. Hold my hand. See how our new cat is good company for us and will not sleep?"

Joseph talked more and Mary less as the hours passed. The three waited. Throughout the night Miri watched, feeling more connected to Mary. She was charmed by the love and admiration she heard for Mary in Joseph's voice, and by the loving tone both shared when they talked about Miri. Something special was happening. Miri could not leave.

It is time.

A little pink-shiny being appeared from Mary and cried, a sharp, loud, determined wail, so different from Miri's own peeping mew. Miri saw waving fists, shining gold from the glow of the flame that had warmed them through the long night.

"Behold our long-awaited Jesus, our son, and the world's son," Joseph rejoiced, and joyously lifted Jesus high into the air. He cleaned him, and wrapped him in the soft folds of worn blankets. He then returned Jesus into Mary's arms.

Miri, watching in fascination, was again caught up

in the shining feeling that she had in her dream. Love, love without beginning or end. This little being was now also hers.

Yet our story does not end here….

It is time.

Chapter V

Even when other human visitors arrived, the warmth, the peace, the happiness never left Miri. She would not leave her station by Mary and baby Jesus as strange men entered the manger, left gifts, admired the baby, and finally left. She also had heard the golden lullabye again, in enchanting tones Joseph now called angelic, and basked again in a dream-like vision, this time in daylight.

Joseph constantly cared for Mary and the baby, feeding her, helping her with baby Jesus. As Mary recovered, she took delight in talking to Miri, inviting her to rest in her bed, near her and Jesus. Mary enjoyed the companionship, and pet Miri in smooth, long strokes. She did not fear Miri being near baby Jesus. She knew the loving care in Miri's heart.

Miri felt special when Mary whispered to her. She knew Mary saw the goodness in Miri—the specialness. It was good…safe…home. Soon Miri's life centered around Mary and her little son. No human had ever shown her such kindness before.

Joseph and Mary shared their meager food supplies with her. Both called to Miri, pet her when she came to them, and loved Miri as much as she loved them.

"She makes me smile. I feel comfort when she sits on my lap and I pet her. Somehow I feel that we are all safe in this little manger."

As Mary spoke these words, Miri saw that she was beautiful to Mary and Joseph. She felt wise, lucky, and as special as they told her she was. She was loved.

And the boy child…Jesus, they called him. He was hers. He had the same shimmer, the same gold glow around him as she had seen in her dream. His pure sweetness filled the stable, and all the animals were soothed.

Jesus was her job, her duty. To watch over him as Ruckey had watched over her. He was Mary's, and Mary loved Miri. Miri must protect him. Yet there was more.

Jesus peered up at Miri as she sat next to his makeshift cradle. Once he even seemed to smile at her. He, too, seemed to know her, and she felt so good when she was near him.

And he was beautiful (as humans go)--silky soft; thick, furry hair; eyes of light. He slept quietly and rarely made those odd sounds he made in the beginning. The new sounds were almost like a kitten's cries. His good, clean, sweet baby smell wafted through the area, blending with the earth and straw scents. Even Fleabit calmed his complaints, and did not stomp anymore. Miri usually slept by his cradle, and soaked in his shining glow. Peace filled the manger. All was well.

One day, the peace would change.

It is time.

Chapter VI

It began as a regular day. Then Joseph did new tasks. Miri watched Joseph as he started packing all their items into bundles. He left to thank Isaac for offering his manger as their haven and to buy supplies. Mary fell asleep, trying to gain her greatest strength for what she knew was to come. Miri and the other animals knew something was about to happen, but could not understand. They only felt the change.

Miri, after a long morning of watching, gradually gave way to her need for sleep. Yet she could not fall into a deep sleep. She catnapped until she heard Kibiddle snort a complaint and the lambs scamper. Something was wrong.

Suddenly she heard a foreign sound. Opening an eye, she thought it might be Tippy, the rabbit, looking for food, scraps from the humans. Then every bit of her fur stood up on end as she realized the source of the sound. It was not Tippy, nor even the small mouse, Ripple. No, instead it was the one she had never wanted to see again, let alone confront.

It is the one that even her mother had feared. One from which she remembered her mother had once fled. One from which Momma Lolly had commanded her kittens to run!

Now the sound turned into a wild snarl. It was Balku, the largest, ugliest, and most fierce of the rat clan. The one Miri, too, had always avoided. Almost as big as the tiny Miri, Balku had the sharpest of teeth, the quickest of claws, the greediest, meanest, darkest slit eyes, and the ugliest of spirits. He was creeping closer and closer to the sleeping baby Jesus. Mary was sleeping. Joseph was gone. Who could save Jesus?

Miri had proclaimed herself as his protector, his guardian. Now she feared she would not be able to defend him. Balku could kill her with one well-placed slash. She never fought a rat before. She always feared fights. Now the strongest combatant of all was moving toward the baby Jesus.

She herself was small, thin, and an inexperienced fighter. She just wanted to run far, far away, and hide from any decision or action. She wanted to protect herself. This was, however, her test. All these thoughts passed behind her saucer eyes. It seemed forever, but it was only a short second. She looked onto her child, Jesus, and his glow filled her from the inside out. She now knew why she was needed.

"It is time," Miri thought.

With more daring and courage than she ever imagined, with more bravery than ever shown by Zori or Ruckey, she leaped in one huge bound to the baby Jesus' cradle, putting herself between the infant and his attacker.

Balku looked at Miri as if she were a fool, a mere inconvenience, but no threat.

Miri, though, felt stronger now than ever before. With a terrifying hiss and mighty swipe of her paw, Miri batted Balku across the cradle to the floor, to immediately get baby Jesus out of danger. Her paws became claws. With another wide, wild leap at Balku, she quickly learned her fighting tactics. A true battle began. Miri used all her might, bound together with her love of Joseph, Mary and baby Jesus. She would not fail. She could not fail.

After many minutes of attacking and being attacked, the battle was finished.
Miri had defeated the rat. He could no longer hurt

anyone. Yet Miri was sorely hurt. She had many horrid bites and cuts. Her beautiful soft fur lay in clumped patches on the ground, and her legs were slashed; they did not easily hold her up. Bleeding, she managed to hobble toward Jesus' cradle. Silently and without complaint, she watched for further danger. Not thinking of her own constant pain, she was determined to not let her eyes lose sight of the precious infant.

Mary had awoken after hearing the first horrid sounds of Miri and Balku fighting, yet there was nothing she could have done to separate them. She had immediately and swiftly taken Jesus into her arms. She had prayed steadily during the rat's snarls and the frightful attack of Balku on Miri. As Miri crawled toward the cradle, Mary crooned softly to her about how wonderfully she had protected Jesus. She showed Miri that Jesus was safe in her arms.

Miri saw Jesus, protected now with Mary, and glimpsed a look in baby Jesus' eyes that seemed to bless her and hold her in the safety of love and understanding. He again gave her a magic smile, not quite a baby's smile, but one most swift and real. Dizzy from her loss of blood, Miri fell to the ground. She knew now that she could die in complete peace, happiness, and fulfillment.

Yet that was not the fate of our little heroine.

Remember what we said about faith and hope?

It is time.

Chapter VII

Joseph returned to find his wife crying over the almost limp body of Miri. He saw the battlefield and the defeated rat. Mary told him of Miri's heroic act. Going swiftly to attend her wounds, Joseph thanked Miri for her willingness to give her life for baby Jesus. He put his home-made salve on Miri, bound up serious injuries the best he could, and prayed.

After placing the cat to rest again at her beloved

station near the baby Jesus, he cleaned the battle area, removed the foe Balku's lifeless remains, sat on the bed with Mary and Jesus, and lead them in another thankful prayer to God, for their safety, for Miri's bravery, and for all the goodness and gifts of life.

To Miri, in her pained, semi-conscious state, the entire room seemed to catch the halo light of baby Jesus, and it again seemed the very sun-star glow of her dream. "It was for this I was born," Miri thought. Her pain now seemed to her to be absorbed by the glow.

A new being appeared, but not with the same feeling and presence of a human. He appeared out of nowhere, covered in the golden-silver glitter Miri had seen with the past glowing visitors at Jesus' birth, in what she had thought was her day dream. The sunshine-moonbeam light spread throughout the room. A "messenger", the being called himself. Joseph called him in a hushed voice, "Angel".

Suddenly the lullaby voice of the angel resounded in the very core of each being in the manger. Again, peace, love. Unimaginable love. Miri could hear and understand every word told to Joseph and Mary. With heads bowed, Mary and Joseph listened to this holy answer from their prayer of thanks.

"Today Miri has become the most blessed of all creatures, for she alone of the animals was willing to give her life for our Lord Jesus. It is for this willing offering that God gives her and all her descendants a gift and a promise. She, and they, will be the most blessed, most special of cats. She and her descendants throughout all generations will pass in lineage the cross of Jesus upon their backs."

"Others throughout the future will continue to see the cross in the cats' physical and spiritual testimonies. Some will bear the cross; others of the line will carry the cross to offspring. A symbol M will also be placed on their foreheads to reveal the opening of the manger, where Miri gave her own offering of love and sacrifice. All who likewise protect and save Miri and all her descendants will be blessed for all time. This is God's promise to Miri."

As the voice echoed throughout the room, Miri felt she would always be loved, and would always have a true family, no matter what came into her future. She would never be alone.

With this promise came Miri's healing. She felt her body soaking in the sun, the love, the happiness. Her wounds began disappearing, and strength returned to her. She had a swift, total healing, one built on the wings and message of an angel.

Was this Miri's happy ending? Would she always be with Mary and Joseph? Change in life is constant, and this was not to be her fate. Yet remember, my children, faith and hope, hope and faith....

It is time.

Chapter VIII

As Mary and Joseph continued readying for their departure, they talked quietly about Miri's future. They knew they could not take her with them on the many difficult journeys ahead, as much as they wanted her. They also loved her and felt responsible for her, especially because Miri had saved Jesus. And had not the Angel given Miri a special promise and blessing?

They wanted the best life for her, but knew few

people in the town. They could not leave her alone in the manger. It weighed on Mary's heart that the little cat that had done so much for them could not stay with her. She could not leave until Miri was safely adopted. She whispered a little prayer for the cat's protection, gave baby Jesus a cuddle, and picked up the cat for a consoling hug.

Suddenly the entrance of the manger was filled with the presence of a very large man with a strong, deep, vibrant voice. It was the local priest James, who cared for a very small congregation near the city center. He did not practice profit from his temple; he was the poor shepherd of his poor flock, yet no man was ever happier. Wearing a faded blue robe, sporting a shaggy huge beard, he still seemed the bright presence of the shining sun as he beamed at the couple, raced across the room, hugged them, blessed baby Jesus, and bid them Godspeed.

Somehow Miri felt this total sunlight of his honest, good, loud presence, and did what she never had before dared to do. She immediately jumped into his arms and purred loudly, allowing him to cradle her on her back like a baby herself. She had never been so bold before, but she knew she was safe. She somehow knew the priest, as she had known Mary and Joseph.

A surprised James was laughing and petting Miri between her ears. After the initial shock, Mary quickly told James how brave Miri had been in saving Jesus. She revealed to him how an angel had appeared, telling them how Miri and her descendants would be blessed through time, and how all protectors will be blessed because of Miri's deed.

Instead of mocking or disbelief, the priest smiled and said (while continuing to pet Miri), "So be it to all sacrifices of love; may these greatest gifts of all be blessed forevermore. It truly humbles me to think this tiny creature can do so much, when we mortals are afraid to dare so much."

"I would be honored," James continued, "to have my temple become the home of such a noble cat.

I will feed her, love her, and spread the story of her strength and dedication to my people. She will have the entire temple as her sanctuary and home. Miri will protect us as we protect her. She and her descendants will be honored. Miri will become a legend to inspire us to become actors based on our love. Her kittens will be given homes where they will be considered blessings upon the family. All who help her continuing family of cats will be blessed; they are special examples and gifts of love to us all."

Miri had no problem going with this man. She felt no sadness leaving the manger, nor even Mary and Joseph. She knew she was carrying Mary, Joseph, and baby Jesus with her in her heart. She had another duty in life, one to continue reminding others of the greatest miracle of all. Loving. Giving love. Trusting. Faith and hope, hope and faith....

So Mary, carrying her precious bundle baby Jesus, walked with James and Miri to the temple to ensure Miri would have a great new home. Joseph stayed at the manger, preparing for the journey.

Thus, my children, Jesus visited the home of his Heavenly Father very early in his life, thanks to Miri. What was ahead for Miri now?

It is time.

Chapter IX

Once inside the little gray stone building, Miri saw all types of people, old, young, small, big, yet she was not scared. She stayed in the arms of James, never thinking of clawing or hurting him. The feeling of complete peace continued to be with her. She knew she would now watch over all these people the way she had Jesus. The little bare temple itself seemed beautiful, so very filled with people praying. All were looking for the same home she had sought.

As she jumped from James' arms, she knew.

"It is time," Miri thought.

She walked the inside boundaries of the musty temple walls, high up on the ledge, patrolling. Miri inhaled the damp, dank, good, earth-smelling air, getting her energy ready for making her new rounds. Miri looked most serious. Making sure all here were safe, protecting her new big family, protecting her new big home. She was needed.

Suddenly she stopped. She smelled something familiar. Damp air, musty earth, animal smells, and that…. Could it be?
A most known smell. Most familiar. A most beloved smell.

She rushed with all her longest leaps to the inner temple floor, where she ran to deliver a twinkling, tiny trill of a sound, and lick the ears of the snoozing small creature before her.

"See?" asked the priest. "She has made herself at

home right away. She has found a new friend, that poor little starved black cat with the broken leg that I found near the outside steps of our temple. That little one had the sweet older cat that looks like Miri—see her over by the rear wall?—next to him. She would not move from his side until I had fixed his leg and given him milk to drink. Now she stays a bit away, usually in the oldest part of the courtyard, but sleeps near him at night."

"I have one other cat too, a spotted black-and-white longhaired boy cat I call Spart. He is mostly a loner who loves the outdoors. Spart plays with the children of the congregation, but does not seem to like other cats. Look, they are all coming to Miri to get to know one another, even Spart!"

So yes, my children…the ears Miri was licking belonged to her beloved brother Ruckey. And the cat who had been constantly by Ruckey's side until he was helped? Miri and Ruckey's own Mama Lolly, who had discovered that life on the streets did not equal her family.

All reunited with great satisfaction. They were a family again, together in a safe place.

The new boy on the block? No one Miri knew, but destined to be her new love, her mate for life. With her, he was no longer a loner. He soon joined the family, then in the next few months decided to come inside the temple, and was known for spending long sessions on the priest's lap while James was studying his sacred books.

Mary and baby Jesus left Miri contentedly purring next to her Momma Lolly, continuously washing Ruckey, and "allowing" Spart to sit near. Mary knew Miri would be secure and happy. She would miss her, but left knowing all would be well.

And so it would. Miri, too, would miss Mary, Joseph, and baby Jesus, but always cherish them in her heart. Yet she has a new chapter, a new duty in her life.

It is time

Chapter X

(How could we leave, Dear Hearts, after Chapter
Nine, when there are so many chapters ahead, for
us, and all Miri's descendants?)

With Spart, Miri produced many litters, many
kittens of many rainbow colors. Every litter or so,
her promise from the angel would visibly return;

the cross that had appeared on her back after the angel visit was carried onto the backs of many of her kittens. The Aramaic form of "M" for manger that had appeared on her own forehead was also apparent on her kittens' foreheads now. Both those marks had appeared on Miri's body suddenly, as soon as the angel had given her the blessing and she had been healed. Now they were being passed on.

And still are....For over two thousand years her descendants, the kittens in her line, have continued the message of that blessing.

For centuries and centuries, until now.

Two thousand years, more leaves than on that maple tree in our front lawn. Generations and generations and generations of manger cats. The forehead "M" continued, and many litters included the very special ones, the ones with the cross carried on their backs. Yet through the centuries, each in Miri's line, cross or no cross, brown-striped or different colors, has been blessed, and has blessed owners and helpers.

The legend of the manger cat has been whispered down by people, from generation to generation, over these two thousand years. Manger cats are considered the luckiest of all cats to have, giving blessings and good luck to all humans who adopt them, protect them, and give them good homes. They were (and still are) known for their unusually serious glance, and their very protective nature toward those that help and love them.

Also, throughout the centuries, stories of unusual, amazing luck and happy events happening to people after they adopt the manger cats abound.

We have experienced those stories of luck ourselves, with our library therapy cat Libby, our soul-full cat Zen, and our present cat, the manger cat, Joanie. These are stories still waiting to be passed down.

And it began with Mary, Joseph, baby Jesus,

James, and his congregation. Yes, the poor congregation of priest James became richer from the luck the manger cats gave them, not just richer in money, but in love and compassion. The story of the gift of the manger cat lifted people's hearts, and made them wish to give sacrifices of love, too. These sacrifices grew as Christ's message spread.

Today the stories of the manger cats continue to be whispered across the continents. Those cats having special understanding for the humans they adopt, those not only protecting their owners, but bringing the best of luck when treated right. Those sitting at bedsides during people's times of pain and suffering, looking into the eyes of the human with love, and wishing to take the pain away and share the joy.

Do you know what made the miracle of the manger cat even more special than the love of a father for his daughter, a girl for her pets, or the love that made an old man young again? Certainly these are also miracles that happened with Miri's sisters and brothers.

The manger cat miracle foreshadowed what Christ has done for us. What Miri was willing to do for Jesus, Jesus has truly done for us all. He has sacrificed His life for us. His love for us made Him die for us on the cross, the very cross that was revealed on Miri's back and the backs of her many descendants. That is why the cross carried on their backs is a reminder of each of our own blessings, given to us by the sacrifice of love.

And thus, my dears, you have my story that I am passing down to you as your legacy…the legend of Miri the Manger Cat, the ancestor of our beloved Joanie the Manger Cat, and all her family descendants to the ends of time. Guard and remember it well.

Remember this story when you see a little kitten or a cat in need…one who needs food, a friendly bit of help, love, a home, a family, as Miri did. Each time that you see our little miracle cat, (the one we found gazing at us with her huge, so-serious, sun-golden eyes from a cage at the local humane shelter), or any of her family, may you remember what you heard in our little bedtime stories.

Remember the sacrifice of Miri and that of the little babe she saved, who Himself saved the world.

Remember hope and faith, and love in action.

It is time.

Afterword: More about Miri

Miri's life continued most happily. Ruckey sensed in her a new strength and dignity, a nobility he had never seen before. They stayed best friends, with a bond that never changed. Miri became the link between Ruckey and Spart; they also became fast friends. With Lolly and other cats, new families emerged…Miri had a family so large she would never be lonely again.

They loved the temple and the congregation. The tastiest gifts of food were constantly brought to them by the children. Many little kittens were adopted into the homes of the most grateful people. Miri and her family continued protecting the congregation; no rat or enemy ever found a place in their homes or the temple. James and his flock in turn protected Miri, her family, and descendants.

Miri lived to be a very old, very wise, and very cherished cat of the congregation. The temple was her forever home. She loved patrolling its ledges and walls while inhaling its great earthy smells, and taught this patrol to her kittens; they continued this custom. The first children Miri guarded so fiercely brought their own children into her presence. These new children loved Miri also, and continued to tell with joy the legend of the manger cat. Thus the whispering of the legend began; this legend continues throughout the generations.

Miri and Spart's kittens all had the serious all-knowing gold eyes of Miri. Many had the brown tiger with black-stripe swirl markings…and the manger "M" on the forehead. Some had crosses, some not. All were special, as special as Miri….

Miri's type of cat would later be called the classic brown tabby. Throughout the centuries and continents, and their multiple varieties of colors, markings, and sizes, these cats continue to be the special loving link from God to the souls of people, the special caregivers to those lucky and wise enough to allow them into their lives.

To all those who love, cherish, adopt, and protect the manger cats, you know already what I mean by blessing and luck. To those who seek them, you need only look as far as the local humane societies, rescue centers, streets, and sometimes even your own doorsteps.

Hope and faith. Faith and hope.
Good luck, and blessings of the manger cats to all!

It is time.